Princess Lya

Princess Lya

Dedication

For my sweet girl,
You are the light that inspired these
stories. Your kindness, joy, and curiosity
remind me daily how precious it is to
teach little hearts with love and grace.
May you always grow in wisdom,
strength, and virtue. Please know how
deeply you are loved.
This is for you, always.

Love,
Mommy

A Note from the Author

"Train up a child in the way he should go, and when he is old he will not depart from it."
—Proverbs 22:6

Tales of Heavenly Manners was born from a longing to plant seeds of virtue in my own daughter's heart and to help other parents do the same in a gentle, joyful, and memorable way.
In a world that moves fast, I believe we need slow moments of storytelling, rooted in timeless truth and character. Through these books, I hope to nurture kindness, respect, patience, and love in little ones everywhere.

This is the second book in a growing series meant to build up young hearts with Biblical values one story at a time. Thank you for joining us on this journey.

With grace,
The Little Seed Library

Acknowledgments

This book was written with love and inspired by my sweet daughter. Watching her grow into a kind, curious, and compassionate little girl has been the greatest blessing, and it's her gentle heart that brought this story to life.

Thank you to my husband who encouraged me along the way, and to every parent, caregiver, and teacher who understands the importance of raising children with grace, faith, and love.

Most of all, I give thanks to God, the King of all kings, who continues to guide my heart as a mother and reminds me that true royalty begins with a heart that reflects His.

May this book be a reminder to little ones everywhere that good manners, rooted in love and kindness, are the mark of a true princess in God's kingdom.

Princess Lya woke up with a smile. A special day had come!
She was going to her friend's house.

She slipped into her new dress, heart fluttering with excitement.

"Mama," said Princess Lya, "I want to be kind and use my best manners."

Her mom replied, "Then do just as Jesus would do. You won't be bringing your Heavenly Manners book today, but you already know what it teaches."

'Let your light shine before others, that they may see your
good deeds and glorify your Father in heaven.'
Matthew 5:16

"Be kind and polite in the way you act. God's gentle ways already shine through you." Mama kindly reminded.

"Remember to say 'please' and 'thank you' and use kind words,"
She continued,
"Be thoughtful and gentle when you are inside someone else's home."

"Be kind and compassionate to one another."
Ephesians 4:32

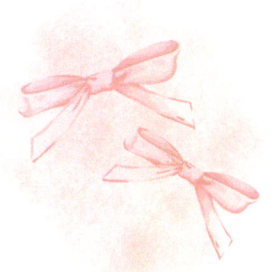

Princess Lya nodded to herself thoughtfully, brushing back her hair beneath her crown.
She carries her Heavenly Manners in her heart,
even if her book stayed at home.

Princess Lya and her mom made their way to her friend JuJu's house full of eager excitement!

At Juju's front door, she slipped off her shoes, because that was the rule in her friend's home. With a cheerful smile she said, "Thank you for having me."

"Do to others as you would have them do to you."
Luke 6:31

Princess Lya remembered to show her manners by not opening up doors she didn't have permission to open. This is not her home so she wanted to be mindful of the family's privacy.

When Juju showed
Princess Lya her toys
and books,
Lya asked kindly, "May I
play with these?"
Juju nodded with a big
smile,
and together they set up
a cozy tea party.

She handled the toys
gently,
never grabbing or
taking without asking.

When Juju's mother
offered to bring them a
snack to share,
Lya said "yes, please".

She also remembered to say
"thank you"
and made sure to clean her
hands before eating.

When playtime was over,
she helped pick up the
toys,
and smiled as she gently
closed the playroom door.

She remembered Colossians 3:23, "Whatever you do, work at it with all your heart, as working for the Lord."

When it was time to leave, she gave hugs and said goodbye.

"Thank you again for the lovely day," she said. Then she walked home with her mom and a heart full of kindness.

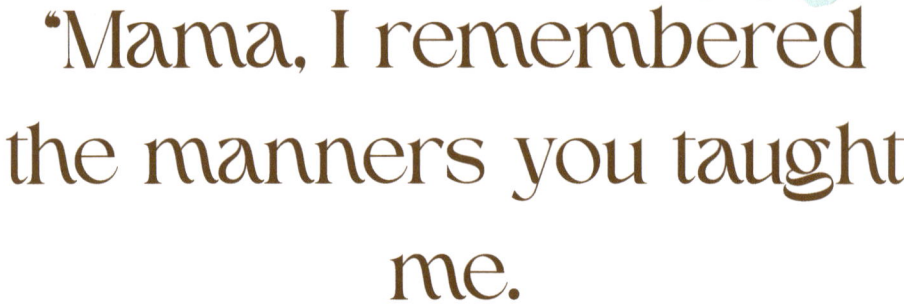

"Mama, I remembered the manners you taught me.
I even thought about the book and the verses.
Even without bringing it, I tried my best, because kindness and respect make others happy."

"Love one another deeply, from the heart."
1 Peter 1:22

Princess Lya's Royal Guest Manners:

- Wait to be invited in
- Greet grown-ups with a smile
- Always say "please" and "thank you"
- Use kind and gentle words
- Ask before touching things that aren't yours
- Follow the house rules
- Respect others privacy by not opening up closed doors
- Play nicely and share
- Help clean up when you're done
- Say sorry if you make a mess or mistake
- Thank your friend and their family before you leave

"I PROMISE TO TRY MY BEST TO SHOW ROYAL MANNERS EVERY DAY!"

SIGNED: _____

Dear Sweet Reader,

Thank you for reading my story! I hope it helped you learn how special and important good manners are. God gave us hearts full of kindness—and when we use them, we shine like royalty!
Always remember: you are loved, you are chosen, and you are a child of the King.

With love,
Princess Lya

"Be kind to one another, tenderhearted, forgiving one another, as God in Christ forgave you."
Ephesians 4:32

THANK YOU FOR READING!

If you enjoyed Princess Lya's Royal Visit, you'll also love the first story in the series: Manners Fit for a Princess

Follow along as Princess Lya continues learning kindness, manners, and heavenly character in her royal adventures!

More Heavenly Manners Tales are coming soon so don't miss them!

Stay connected with me for updates, new book releases, and special extras:

@Brytcreates

TikTok

Instagram